KNITWITS

Also by William Taylor:

Agnes the Sheep
Paradise Lane

KNITWITS

William Taylor

SCHOLASTIC
HARDCOVER

Scholastic Inc.
New York

Library of Congress Cataloging-in-Publication Data

Taylor, William, 1940–
  Knitwits / William Taylor.
      p.   cm.
  Summary: Charlie Kenny's life becomes chaotic when
he gets himself into a bet that he can knit something for the baby
his mother is expecting.
      ISBN 0-590-45778-0
  [1. Family life — Fiction.   2. Schools — Fiction.   3. Knitting —
Fiction.   4. Sex roles — Fiction.]   I. Title.
PZ7.T2187Kn   1992
[Fic] — dc20   91-46241
                                                                      CIP
                                                                      AC

12 11 10 9 8 7 6 5 4 3 2   3 4 5 6 7/9

Printed in the U.S.A.   37

First Scholastic printing, September 1992

For my good friends
Anthea and Bill Tidswell

KNITWITS

1

Our cat croaked this morning.

I got tossed off our hockey team this afternoon.

Then, to top things off, Mum told me she was going to have a baby.

It was one of those days!

It started with the cat.

"He got hit by a truck," I told the guys. "It was speeding."

"Wasn't speeding fast enough," said Spikey. "Did you see it?"

"The truck was speeding," I said. "Not the cat."

"Yeah. Reckon the cat wasn't," said Spikey. "Was it traumatized?"

"No. It was squashed flat."

"Yep. That's traumatized, I think. Was its guts hanging out?"

I did little bites on my tongue and my lips. "Yep. They sure were."

"Where is it?" asked Jacko.

"In our garden. We buried it."

"Can we come home with you after school, Chas?

So's we could dig him up and have a look at him."

"Nah. Mum wouldn't like it. She got all upset. She's planted a tree on top of him now."

"Lucky tree," said Spikey. "Sure gonna have a good feed."

Mr. Magoo was our cat. He was the same age as me. Dad found him as a little kitten on our doorstep when he got home from having a first look at me. "Couldn't get rid of it, could I?" he always said. "Not on that day and me feeling all soft and warm inside." So he took it in and gave it a saucer of milk, and it stayed for the whole of my life until today.

Dad always said he hated cats. "Sly, cunning things. Can't trust 'em." I just reckon it was nice Mr. Magoo never found this out. He was always Dad's cat. For someone who hated cats, my dad sure gave this one a lot of love. Mr. Magoo was no easy cat to love. He had a real mean streak, a set of claws he loved to exercise and, boy, was he ugly! Grandma always said it was a toss-up who was the ugliest — Mr. Magoo as a kitten, or me as a baby and if she'd had her way she'd have got rid of both of us. I think she was only joking.

So we buried Mr. Magoo. Mum and me wrapped him up real nice in one of our good towels. "Mr. Magoo only ever liked the best," she said. Mum cried quite a lot. So did I. Mr. Magoo sure got buried in a wet good towel. Dad dug the hole. He dug so fast he kept on getting dirt in his eyes and had to stop and wipe them all the time. Or that's what he says.

Then Mum made Dad dig up a bush she'd planted somewhere else. We planted it again — on top of Mr. Magoo.

When I went back to school after lunch, I got tossed right off our hockey team and it wasn't even me who swore in the first place. "Didn't say nuthin' at all, Ms. Mason-Dixon," I said.

"Anything, Charles," said Ms. Mason-Dixon, our teacher and our hockey coach rolled into one. "Just count yourself lucky I don't put you out for the season."

"What do you think you heard him say, Ms. Mason-Dixon?" asked Alice Pepper, who sits right next to me and is captain of our hockey team.

"You keep out of this, Alice Pepper," said Ms. Mason-Dixon. "It's none of your business."

"I think we got a right to know exactly what he said, Ms. Mason-Dixon," said Alice. " 'Coz I, for one, don't want Charlie Kenny polluting the air I breathe with his dirty bad language and I want to know what sort of pollution it is. I'm the captain of the team, too."

For sure Alice Pepper should know what sort of pollution it was! It was her, not me, who had done the polluting.

What a day! So, what else could happen? I'll tell you what!

Mum and Dad cooked a good big dinner to cheer

us up. "It's Mr. Magoo's funeral dinner," said Mum. "He would've liked it."

This was very true. For the first time ever we got to eat everything ourselves from our plates. Mr. Magoo had never eaten cat food. He had no taste for it at all and he spewed it up. For years and years Mr. Magoo had eaten the best bits from our plates. If you didn't give them to him he just jumped up and took them. If you tried locking him out he yowled at the top of his enormous lungs until you let him in again.

I started to see that Mr. Magoo, underground, could have good advantages over Mr. Magoo up on top of the ground.

Then we had a look at the Mr. Magoo photos. There were sure heaps of them. I think Mum and Dad have more photos of Mr. Magoo than they do of me. Mum wanted to pick one out to put in a frame. There were a lot to choose from. There was Mr. Magoo swimming in the bath. (Mr. Magoo had always enjoyed a good swim.) There was one of Mr. Magoo bullying a very large German shepherd dog. There was Mr. Magoo up a power pole, and a fireman and Grandma climbing up a fire-engine ladder to rescue him. Mr. Magoo wearing a hat. Mr. Magoo out duck hunting in the park. Mr. Magoo reading a good book and wearing glasses. And so on.

Mum finally chose one of Mr. Magoo and Dad —

asleep and sunbathing out in the backyard and each with a can of beer just by their paws. She took a nice shot of me and Grandma out of her best frame and put Dad and Mr. Magoo in. "Mum wouldn't mind," she said. "Not under the circumstances."

"Wouldn't bet on it, sugar," said Dad. "Still, don't you worry. She'll blame me, so it's all right."

Then the blow fell.

"We weren't going to tell you, Chas," said Mum. "Not just yet. But because of what's happened to Mr. Magoo, and your hockey team, too, Dad and me think you need one little ray of sunshine in your day. Something to make you feel better."

"It's OK, Mum," I said. "I'm OK."

"There's going to be a new little arrival in our family," she said.

"We getting a new cat?"

"Not quite," said Mum.

"Can we get a dog this time?"

"I don't think you quite understand, love," said Mum, and she patted her middle. "My little Chas is going to have to learn how to share."

"Eh?"

"There's going to be the patter of another pair of tiny feet," said Mum, and I think she sort of blushed a bit. "Not that yours are all that tiny anymore, and certainly not when you've got your hockey boots on."

"Liz, for heaven's sake!" Dad said to Mum and then he turned to me. "What your mother's trying to tell you, Chas," said Dad, "is that she's . . . er . . ."

"Pregnant," I said.

2

She's far too old, is Mum. I've told her it's a danger at her time of life. She should have had something done about it before it was too late. On health grounds, that is.

"I'm only twenty-nine, Chas," she said to me.

As if that isn't too old! I ask you!

"Women today are having babies well into their forties," said Mum.

"The guys'll laugh at me having a baby," I said.

"You're not having the baby, Chas," she said. "Spikey's mum's got three younger than him and Jacko's mum's the next best thing to fifty."

"Yeah, but he hasn't got a baby," I said.

"He *is* the baby," said Mum.

"Grandma won't like it," I said.

"Well . . ." began Mum. "We, Dad and me, and now you . . . we won't be telling Grandma for just a little while yet."

"Scared, eh?" I gave a little laugh. "You'll have to tell her when you start to show."

"Huh! My word. You do know all about it," Mum smiled.

"And that won't be long if you've got your times all right and you are just over halfway through. It's now as big as a couple of bananas."

"Whew!" said Mum.

"You know what Grandma always says," I started.

"You don't have to believe everything Grandma always says," said Mum.

"She's always said you got one kid too many already and it's wrecked your life and your great promise and all that. Now what's she going to say when you tell her you're going to double your number of kids?"

Mum suddenly laughed and she gave me a bit of a punch. "It's not a problem," she said. "She'll blame Daddy."

"Well," I said, looking at her. "He did have something to do with it."

"Now you sound like Grandma," said Mum.

A long long time ago my mother, Elizabeth, and my father, James (Liz and Jim), were the boy and girl next door. They were childhood sweethearts. They reckon (and who am I to disagree because I wasn't around back then and don't know) they never even went out with anyone else. Not ever. Not once.

Mum is supposed to be a great beauty. You wouldn't think so to look at her. She has a famous face and figure and uses them sometimes to get us out of trouble with the bank manager and the mortgage when Dad's out of work. Dad's a carpenter and he's always getting laid off because of downturns in the building industry. "Laid-off, be damned!" Grandma often says. "You've been sacked, James. Yet again!"

So Mum's great beauty is quite useful. She's a model who gets photographed for magazines and gets used in telly ads for all sorts of junk. At home or in the garden or down at the shops, you'd just never guess. Mum says this is just the way she wants it and it suits her fine. Dad says he'd like just a few more guys around the place to know he is married to a famous sex symbol. At home Mum wears old clothes, ties her hair back with a bit of string, never ever wears makeup, and can look even older than her mum, my grandma.

Alice Pepper reckons my mum pays a stand-in to do the ads and the photos for her. "Your mum's not beautiful at all," she often tells me. "In fact, she's very, very ugly."

"She's not ugly," I usually say.

"My mum says your mum's eyes are too close together and she's got a long nose and too big hips and hair like the mane of an old moldy lion."

"Your mum looks like a dingo," I said from the other side of a fence. "She looks like an old dingo dog crossed with a buffalo."

"My mum says looks are not important," said Alice Pepper.

"Just as well," I said. "For you and for her."

When I told Mum she just laughed. "Poor Maureen. Guess it's time I had her over for a cup of tea. It's just that it's really so boring — Alice has always given me a far more interesting account of their news."

The boy and girl next door!

Childhood sweethearts!!

This is one big worry and a problem.

My next-door neighbor is Alice Pepper! Alice Pepper is my girl next door!!

My problem is that if God Almighty was holding His great right arm and His great right fist up above me and yelling down at me that he'll traumatize me if I don't tell the truth, then I'd have to admit that it's not Spikey and it's not Jacko who are my best friends. Nor is it any other guy. My best friend is Alice Pepper. The only living soul I'd ever admit this to is God Almighty and that's because I fear Him almost as much as I fear Alice Pepper.

Alice Pepper has been two months older than me since we were born. She's been my girl next door as long as I've lived. She's bossed me around as long as I've lived! There are some quite wrong people like Ms. Mason-Dixon, our teacher, who say we even look alike. "Like two peas in a pod," she says. Me! An Alice Pepper look-alike!! The very thought of it can send deep shudders up and down my spine.

There is nothing nothing nothing about Alice Pepper and me that looks alike. We may be the same shortish size. We may be sort of the same squarish shape. Of course we do both have blue eyes and we both have a lot of freckles and that awkward sort of dark brown hair that flops forward all the time and into your eyes. We both play hockey. We both have a lot of scars on bits of our bodies from where we've played hockey. We both lost our first teeth at the same time and then ended up with second sets that look a bit big and fill up half our faces. But apart from that we don't look alike at all. Not one little bit!

3

Do I wish to share my life with a baby?

The answer is a flat no, and I'm not being selfish at all.

He'll be into nicking everything I own and want all my things in no time flat. In no time flat he'll be after all my stuff. In no time flat he'll be into my T-shirts and sweatshirts and even think he's big enough to fit my jeans and sneakers.

Grandma says having a baby is a bit like a raffle and she's hoping Mum will come up with a better prize the second time around, and doesn't Mum think she's bought one too many tickets already. Grandma says she can't understand why she seems to have been the last to be told the happy news.

Alice Pepper has confirmed my very worst unspoken fears. The baby could be a girl! "Least then I'd have someone sensible to talk to and share secrets with. It's all boys round here and that's pure puke. My mum knew your mum was pregnant."

"She did not so."

"She did."

"She didn't."

"She did. She told me. She said she saw your mum was getting as fat round the middle as she already is round her bum. She said you could even tell it in that ad on the telly where she wears next to nothing and tips all that milk down that guy's throat and says 'Cool as . . . Cool as milk,' in what she thinks is a sexy voice. She could even tell in that ad."

"Mum did that one last year and wasn't even pregnant then unless ladies are pregnant for just about two years and that's impossible," I said.

"No it's not and elephants are and Mum says she could tell your mum was going to try and get pregnant and it was written all over her. What you going to make for your baby?" asked Alice.

"Nuthin'."

"You've got to," said Alice Pepper. "It's the law. It'll be your little sister. You're gonna be the poor little devil's brother."

"It'll be my brother."

"It's a girl," said Alice Pepper. "I can always tell."

"I'm gonna knit him a sweater," I said.

"You're gonna WHAT!!!?"

"You heard me," I said. But why why why had I said it? Why? I must be double mad. Can I knit? Of course I can't knit! Alice Pepper does that sort of thing to me. Still, everyone knits junk for poor babies. Why not me?

"You? Knit? Bet you don't."

"Bet I do. I just bet I can knit something for a baby," I said.

"Bet you can't."

"How much d'you bet?"

"A thousand million trillion dollars," said Alice Pepper.

"You haven't got that much."

"Yeah. And you can't knit, either. I know. So there!" said Alice Pepper. "So I'll bet all my collections, every one of them, every single one of them, that you can't knit your baby a sweater."

Wow! WOW!! Alice Pepper is one bigtime collector. Alice Pepper has got a bottle top collection, a beer can collection, a paper napkin collection, a light bulb collection, a matchbox collection, a dead insect collection, and an old coin collection. Alice Pepper has also got the prize collection of all, the most brilliant and awesome collection of all — a skull collection.

Alice Pepper owns the skulls of a sparrow, a starling, a parrot, a mouse, a rat, a chicken, a duck, a rabbit, a possum, a cat, a dog, a hare, a sheep, a goat (with horns), a horse, a deer (with one horn), and a cow (with half a horn). Alice Pepper says it's only a matter of time before she gets hold of the skulls of a monkey and a human, and she's working on both. Well, I know it's only a matter of time for the human one. Alice Pepper has told me that after about a hundred years human skulls that have been buried with their owners start popping up to the surface in cemeteries. Once they've left the rest of their owner they're anyone's. Our cemetery is about a hundred years old and we go there quite often, her and me, just to check if the first skull has popped up. So far it hasn't.

"And when you lose, which you will, you can give me five dollars a week for the rest of my life and no matter how long I live," said Alice Pepper.

"I don't get five dollars a week," I said.

"Then I'll just put it all down in a notebook until you do, even if you go on the dole and you probably will," said Alice Pepper. "And I'm gonna charge you interest."

"You're on," I said, and stuck out my hand.

"Oh, no no no. You don't get away with it easy as that," said Alice. "This is a big one, a very big one. You gotta shake three times!"

So we shook hands three times and swore we'd go to hell and get our throats slit if we told a lie about it.

"Aaaahhhh . . ." Alice Pepper let out a big satisfied sigh. "Five bucks a week for life. Always knew you were a sucker and now you proved it. Like taking money from a baby, and I reckon that's sort of what I am doing."

"Don't you bet on it, Pepper," I said, and jumped the hedge that separates our houses in some places. "I can so knit. I can knit real good."

"No you can't, sucker. So there. And you never

ever will. Five bucks a week for life, sucker."

"It's gonna be a surprise and don't you tell no one I'm knittin' a sweater. Not the guys. Not Jacko and Spikey."

"Wouldn't tell them their faces look like the bum of an ape and they do," said Alice Pepper.

Alice Pepper did not like the guys. The guys did not like Alice Pepper. The only living creature who could beat Jacko and Spikey and me in anything, even in a fight, was Alice Pepper, my girl next door.

4

With the baby coming Dad has had to give up smoking. He's finding it a bit hard. Mum says it's just about OK if he stands out in the middle of the backyard, but even then it could be bad for our fetus.

"No smoke or fumes are going to harm this kid," said Mum, patting her belly. Even I can see Mum is now a bit fatter.

"Pardon me for breathing," said Dad. "Didn't seem to hurt the last one. What are you going to do about the fire in the lounge?" he asked. Our lounge fire smokes worse than Dad ever did.

"You're going to fix it, dear," said Mum. "You're the carpenter in the family."

"That's cool," said Dad. "At the same time I'll get on to the local council and get them to stop all the traffic up and down our street for the next few months."

"Why, dear?"

"The poisonous fumes, that's why," he said, and

went out into the middle of the backyard.

I joined him. "Tell you what, Chas, you'n me'll share the biggest, fattest, richest cigar I can find when this damn baby's born. That's what us guys are supposed to do."

"Choice," I said, looking forward to the day.

"You shouldn't be helping him to smoke, Mr. Kenny," came the voice of Alice Pepper from under a hedge. "Can I have one, too?"

"Sure, Alice," said Dad.

"Did you have a big, fat, and rich cigar when he was born?" She pointed at me. "Not that you got anything much to be happy about and you probably just wanted to have a good cry."

"Started one, Alice. I remember that. Then Mr. Magoo the kitten began choking, and I put it out and never found it again. Should've gone on smoking and finished him off back then. I hate cats." He looked over at Mr. Magoo's tree and was quiet for a moment. "Poor old boy."

"You working just now, Mr. Kenny? Or you been laid off again?" asked Alice.

"Yeah, I'm working, Alice. Doing up a house for an old lady."

"Good one. Then you could start on yours. It sure needs it," said Alice Pepper. "I'm glad you got some work 'coz they won't want Mrs. Kenny for any more ads, eh, and you'll have to be on the dole."

"It's a hard life, Alice," said Dad.

"Why are you standing in the middle of your

backyard, Mr. Kenny?" asked Alice. "It's getting dark."

"Mind your own business, Alice Pepper," I said. "It's our backyard and we can stand all over it whenever we like."

"Guess you're just thinking about Mr. Magoo and missing him. You have my real deep sympathy, Mr. Kenny, for Mr. Magoo getting squashed and traumatized," said Alice Pepper. "I'm sorry I didn't get to be invited to the funeral for him."

"Thank you, Alice," Dad said. "There wasn't time for invitations."

"In a while can I dig up his skull if it's not traumatized too bad?" asked Alice Pepper. "For my collection?"

"Over my dead body, Alice," said Dad.

"Tee, hee hee hee hee . . . then I could get yours, too, Mr. Kenny. Good one," said Alice.

How can I get to learn to knit? How? How? How? As sure as my name is Charles Patrick Kenny, I am not going to spend the rest of my life keeping Alice Pepper in great luxury, and I've never been one to go back on a bet. For all that I may not want a baby around the place, I most certainly do want Alice Pepper's skull collection. She can keep all the rest of her junk. I just want those skulls!

The town library was no help. *The Complete Encyclopedia of Knitting* looked quite interesting.

Seems that knitting has been around just about forever and has even been dug up on Egyptian mummies. But the book didn't let on how those mummies learned to knit.

The Bonnie Baby Boutique was of a bit more help. They had a heap of pattern books for baby booties, blankets, jackets, sweaters, and hats. You could tell all this from the pictures. But have you ever tried to read one? They seem to be written in another language. They may tell you what to do but they don't seem to tell you how to do it.

Ask Mum? No. I'm doing this one by myself and I want it to be a big surprise for Mum as well as for our baby.

Ask Dad? Well, my dad can do a lot of things but I don't think I've ever seen him sit down for a nice knit. Anyway, he'd sure tell Mum.

Ask Grandma? If all else fails I'll just have to. To be very honest, Grandma and me get on each other's nerves a bit. We are happiest, and like each other most, when we are apart. When Grandma is not blaming Dad for stuffing up her daughter's life, she's blaming me. As if I've ever had any choice in the matter.

I don't think Jacko and Spikey can knit. Well, I know they can't because I know everything about them and what they can do. They sure couldn't knit without me knowing and I'd give them both heaps if I caught them doing it. I know they'd give me heaps if they caught me at it. We're like that, the three of us. Spikey and Jacko are quite interested in our baby.

"My old lady says your old lady's in the club," said Spikey in Ms. Mason-Dixon's class one day.

"My old lady's in what club?" I asked. The only club I knew Mum belonged to was the garden club.

"He's not letting on, eh?" said Jacko. "And we're his very best mates. Your old lady's got one in the oven."

"What they're trying to say, thick brick," said Alice Pepper, who was walking by, "is that your mother is pregnant."

"Bug off, Alice Pepper," I said. "I knew that."

"You didn't."

"I did. Now bug off. It was supposed to be a secret."

"Not much of a secret when you're just about the size of an outsize hippo, nitwit," and she winked at me. "Nitwit," she repeated, slowly.

"Stuff off, Pepper," I said.

"I'm going," she said, and she was gone.

"Why they want another kid?" asked Spikey. "They're nuts. They got more'n enough with just you."

I think Spikey must have been thinking of his three younger sisters and who could blame him.

"I wouldn't mind a kid brother or even a sister," said Jacko. "Then I'd have something to boss around and do all the work instead of me."

I think Jacko must have been thinking of all his older sisters. Jacko says he's their slave.

"I reckon your old lady must've forgotten to take her pill," said Spikey. "My old lady did that with our baby. That's what she says."

"Or your old man might've forgotten to use something," said Jacko. "That can happen, too."

"My old lady and my old man are gonna have a baby because they want to have a baby," I said firmly. "And we are all, well, sort of pleased about it. Well, I dunno if my old lady's old lady is all that pleased but she's not having it, is she?" I finished.

"Your life will never be the same," Spikey shook his head.

"Sure won't," Jacko shook his.

"Maybe now, after that highly interesting and informative discussion, we could all get back to our mathematics," said Ms. Mason-Dixon. "To the very best of my knowledge we are not doing multiplication today. Or are we?" She stared down on us with that tough look that she has.

I stared back up at her. "Can you, er . . . er . . . doesn't matter, Ms. Mason-Dixon."

"Can I do what, Charles? Don't you know by now, Charles, I can do most anything? Girls can, you know."

As sure as chickens come out of eggs, Ms. Mason-Dixon was no longer a girl. However, if, as she said, she could do most anything, as sure as chickens come out of eggs she must be able to knit.

So I stayed behind after school.

5

"Can you teach me something and keep it a dead secret, Ms. Mason-Dixon?" I asked. "Like in a hurry."

"If I've managed to teach you anything at all so far, Charles, it's certainly been kept a dead secret. What d'you have in mind? Shoot! I've got an appointment at your grandma's gym."

Ms. Mason-Dixon is a tough old bird. That's what I've heard my Dad say and I couldn't disagree. Ms. Mason-Dixon taught both my mum and dad. Ms. Mason-Dixon and Grandma are good friends because both of them are feminists and into fitness.

"It's gotta be a secret," I said.

"Don't look at me with those great round eyes as sweet and innocent as a lamb. Your father used to try the same tricks and it might've fooled your poor mother but it never worked on me. What d'you want?"

"I want to learn to knit."

"Now I've heard everything," said Ms. Mason-Dixon.

"Mum's having this baby and I want to knit it a sweater and you're the very very best person I can think of to show me how to do it." I smiled at her nicely.

"Tell that to the birds. I'm probably the only poor mug you can think of," said Ms. Mason-Dixon. "Just as big a con man as your father. Tell me, is he still out of work?"

"Nope. He's doing up an old lady's house."

"Poor old soul. Hope she knows what she's let herself in for. Get him to give me a call. I want a wall knocked out and a couple of windows put in and I haven't the time to do it myself. Might as well put a few days' work his way," said Ms. Mason-Dixon.

"OK. How about the knitting?"

"What's behind all this?" she asked.

So I told her most of it.

"Alice Pepper, eh?" Ms. Mason-Dixon grinned at me. "All right. I'll do what I can. God knows I'm not the world's best knitter. What do I get in return?"

"Eh?"

"Fair's fair, Charles. Here I am about to spend goodness knows how much time in what is likely to be a useless effort to teach you an old, old art form — and you're certainly not a quick learner as far as I can see. Fair's fair. Four lawn mows."

"Done."

"Four hours of weeding?"

"No," I said. "Four lawn mows, Ms. Mason-Dixon. Fair's fair, Ms. Mason-Dixon."

"Was worth a try," she said. "You drive a hard bargain."

I drive a hard bargain? "Can you put me back on our hockey team, Ms. Mason-Dixon?" It seemed a good moment to try when she seemed to be a bit softer than usual. "I missed the game Saturday."

"No," said Ms. Mason-Dixon. "You shouldn't have sworn."

"I didn't."

"I know that, Charles. You know that, Charles. Alice Pepper knows that, Charles. But, boy, until one of you decides to tell the truth, that's the way things are."

"It's not fair."

Ms. Mason-Dixon gave a short sort of laugh like a bark. "Who ever said anything about fair? Tomorrow, after school, my place. And you haven't missed playing one Saturday, Charles. Not yet. It rained last weekend. Remember?"

A very tough old bird indeed.

Alice Pepper is going to build our baby a tree-house. "She'll need somewhere to get away from you, and she and me can have our talks up there."

"Babies can't climb trees," I told her. "How's she going to get up there?"

"I'll carry her over my shoulder," she said. "I'll use the fireman's lift. No sweat. Here, I'll show you," and she hoisted me over her shoulder and took me for a walk round the garden.

"You haven't got any wood," I said. "You can't build a treehouse without wood."

"Your dad's got heaps. Mum says he's nicked it from jobs he's been sacked from. It's all under your house."

"It's for finishing off our house one day, and he hasn't nicked it."

Like my mum never looks like a model round our house or down at the shops, well, my dad never looks like a builder and carpenter, either. We have the most unfinished house on our street. One of our rooms hasn't even got a floor but it's going to have one soon because it's the baby's room. It was Mr. Magoo's room before he croaked because it meant he could be either inside or outside depending on his mood.

Grandma tells Dad he's as lazy as all get out and her daughter should not have to live in an unfinished house. Dad just grins at her. Then she asks whatever does he do all day when he's been sacked and doesn't he know the devil makes work for idle hands? Dad just grins again and tells her he lazes around, having a good time and drinking and smoking and watching videos with his out-of-work mates. Grandma says she knows this quite well and it's not good enough.

It doesn't worry Mum at all that the house is not finished. Mum says she's not the best housekeeper in the world and the less house there is to keep the better she's pleased. It gives her more time to spend in her garden. Mum loves her garden very much.

Alice Pepper says our baby's treehouse is going to be up one of their trees. "I don't want any problems of who owns it when you all get chucked out of your place," she said.

"We're not gonna get chucked out of our place," I said to her.

"You will be, my mum says. You're so behind with the mortgage you're going to get chucked out any day by the bank manager and the cops. That's what Mum says."

"Bull," I said. This is a very good word of Dad's. He says it doesn't count as swearing these days.

"It's true," said Alice Pepper.

"Well you better build the treehouse big and we can all move up there," I said.

"No way," said Alice Pepper. "That treehouse is just for the baby and me. She'n me won't let anyone up there. Not even your mum."

"You'll have to let Mum up," I said. "Unless you can breast-feed a baby, Alice Pepper, and I know you can't do that because you haven't got any boobs. Mine are bigger'n yours and I don't think I could feed a baby."

6

"Where's your wool, Charles? Where are your knitting needles, boy? Pattern? No? So, you're expecting me to provide the lot, eh? Five lawn mows, I think. Maybe six. How d'you take your tea?"

"A lot of milk and three sugars, Ms. Mason-Dixon." I didn't think it was a good time to tell her I'd rather have coffee. "Thank you very very much indeed. This is very very kind of you to give me up your spare time."

"Little greaser," said Ms. Mason-Dixon, and got down to work. After a while she said, "I can see what your grandma means about you."

After an hour I think Ms. Mason-Dixon was feeling very very sorry she had given up her spare time. Ms. Mason-Dixon seemed just about at the point of pulling out her short gray hair. "I've always said, Charles, yours is just about the slowest learning family I've ever taught. Your mother, your father, your aunts, your uncles, the whole lot of you. And you, Charles, are not giving me any reason to think things are changing for the better. You all seem to think that learning is a matter of just sitting there and smiling sweetly and that, suddenly, out of the blue, it'll all come to you. . . . What have I done to deserve this?"

"I done it!" I said, looking at my ten stitches of knitting. "I think I'm getting down to it." It sure looked OK to me. I better calm her down. I still needed a little bit of help.

"Done what, boy? Getting down to what? You've turned a nice little piece of white wool into a thick, gray, greasy, grubby knot."

"I think I'm nearly getting it," I said.

"D'you want another cup of tea?" Ms. Mason-Dixon asked. "Let's see where you're up to. Into the sort of back . . . wool around . . . back we come, nice and careful . . . over and out. Into the back again . . . I think I need something stronger than tea. You've got fingers like dead sausages, Charles," she said, shaking her gray head.

"To the best of my knowledge, Ms. Mason-Dixon, all sausages are dead sausages," I said.

"Your fingers are deader than most," said Ms. Mason-Dixon.

Ms. Mason-Dixon had a beer and I had a Coke. "Tell you what, Charles. You finish your drink and then take off. Work at it tonight — maybe you'd better not go to bed at all — and come back and see me tomorrow afternoon after school."

"Can I play hockey for our team on Saturday, please Ms. Mason-Dixon?"

"No. Now get out. My head's splitting," she said.

I don't know why her head was splitting. I hadn't done anything. It wasn't my fault. Into the sort of back down the bottom in the middle . . . wool around . . . loop it off and . . . piece of cake this knitting. Piece of cake, all right. It grows, too. Not only downwards but outwards. I started with only ten little loops down the bottom. Now I got sixteen! Sure is a piece of cake.

Mum says she's going to call our baby Alexandra if it's a girl (which it won't be), or Alexander if it's a boy. Dad says if the baby's anything like him and Mum once were then it won't be able to spell its name until it's just about fifteen. "We'll call it Jo," he said. "Can't go wrong with Jo. Even I can spell Jo."

"No baby of mine is going to be called Jo," said Mum.

Alice Pepper has offered to sell us her name. "My name is copyright," she told me. "That means no one can steal it off me. But because it'll be your sister and we're next-door neighbors and I like your mum and dad and they like me, I'm willing to give them a good deal."

"Like what sort of deal?" I asked. "Five bucks a week for the rest of your life?" I think Alice Pepper was more to worry about than the bank manager and the mortgage.

I couldn't think of anything worse than calling our baby Alice Pepper. It is only someone like Alice Pepper's mum who would have thought of it in the first place. "It won't work, anyway," I told her. "Think of the trouble it would cause for the postman. They wouldn't know which Alice Pepper to give a letter to. To you or to ours. Won't work."

"I would be Alice Pepper I, and your baby would be Alice Pepper II. It's done all the time," she said. "You seen *The Terminator* on telly? Well, you got *Terminator* and you got *Terminator II*. I seen them both."

"It's gonna be right funny if it's a boy. You can't call a boy Alice Pepper. Think of what the other guys'd say to it at school."

Alice Pepper said five swearwords in a row and then, "That's the least of my problems, and you can call a baby anything you like and that's the law. Besides, my mum doesn't think your mum'll go full term. That's nine months, is full term. She'll lose it. Mum says this often happens with change-of-life babies. Your mum's old and she's been out of practice for too long. Looking at you I reckon you probably stuffed up all her insides when you were in there. Look at you! If it comes too soon and it's dead you can bury it down the back by Mr. Magoo and don't forget to ask me to the funeral this time."

Mum has said no to Alice Pepper's offer of her name. "Couldn't afford it, dear," she told me. "Not with Dad in and out of work. And as Alice has told you, they'll never want me on the telly again. Not after this," she patted her stomach.

Mum says that at the age of twenty-nine she may not be a spring chicken anymore but she's hardly over the hill and her insides are all OK and in tip-top order. "Popped you out like a pea out of a pod. No reason to think Alexandra won't pop out the same way," she said.

"Jo," said Dad.

"Alexandra," said Mum, who is going to have a talk to Mrs. Maureen Pepper about something called old wives' tales.

"I know what I want our baby called," I said.

"What, dear?" asked Mum.

"Let's hear it," said Dad. "Couldn't be any worse than Alexandra."

"Munro," I said.

Mum and Dad looked at each other. They said nothing.

"Yep. Reckon Munro is a right cool name for a baby," I said.

"You might have to wait to use it till you've got one of your own," said Dad.

"Why Munro?" asked Mum. "I don't think . . ."

"It's not hard to spell. It's got a good right sort of sound to it. I've always liked it for a baby's name," I said.

"First time I've heard of it," said Dad. "You've never said so before."

I gave him a hard look. "There's been no need to, has there? The last baby we had was me. You sure didn't give me a chance to choose back then. Alice Pepper says you can change your own name if you want to. If you don't want Munro for our baby, well, I just might be changing mine."

Munro. Munro. Sounds right good. I'm going to knit Munro a sweater. I just know it in my bones that Munro Kenny is going to be wearing a sweater knitted by his older brother.

7

"Charles," said Ms. Mason-Dixon, who was on her second beer. (We no longer bother much with the tea.) "You've got about as much chance of becoming a knitter as I have of becoming a bull-fighter."

"Gee, Ms. Mason-Dixon, you really going to become a bullfighter? That's very, very interesting." I now find it helps to chat while you knit. The chatting soothes the knitting. "A bullfighter? Very interesting indeed." Poor bull!!

This was my fourth visit and, strange as it may seem, Ms. Mason-Dixon and me are becoming quite close friends — in a knitting sense. The great art of knitting is the thing we have in common and it has pulled us together in friendship. She has been a great help to me. "You'll have to go to Spain, Ms. Mason-Dixon. That's where the bulls are for the fighting," I said to her. One part of me jumped with joy. This sure was a great way of getting rid of Ms. Mason-Dixon from our school for good, specially if the bull won. The other part of me felt a bit mean. In her own home, with all her own things around her and just me and no other kids, Ms. Mason-Dixon was certainly a top-quality knitting teacher and almost a human being. She drives the hard bargain! I'm now up to ten lawn mows.

"This is it, Charles. After this you're on your own," said Ms. Mason-Dixon. "You won't knit a jersey for your baby in a month of nonhockey-playing Saturdays. Why don't you settle for knitting a nice hankie — for its teddy bear. I'd help you." She handed me a shoe box.

"I'll knit him a sweater. I really will. You must have faith, Ms. Mason-Dixon," I said.

"It'll take more than faith, Charles. It'll take a bloody miracle, excuse my French."

" 'Bloody' isn't French, Ms. Mason-Dixon, but you can say it if you like and I won't tell," I said, and opened the box. Wow! The dear old lady had packed away for me a box full of balls of wool of all sorts of colors. On top of the balls were three pairs of brand-new metal knitting needles. It is good you can get ones you can't break. The plastic ones are like little matchsticks in my fingers.

"You're on your own, man. Just remember, come back to me for help any time you like, and every time you come back is one more lawn mow."

Seemed like it was one big toss-up which was worse. Keep Alice Pepper in luxury for life or mow

Ms. Mason-Dixon's lawns forever. "On my own it is, Ms. Mason-Dixon. Thank you very very much. Knitting's cool as."

"Cool as what, Charles?"

"Tell you what, Ms. Mason-Dixon, and it's only fair after all you done for me, after I done this one for our baby guess what I'm gonna do?"

"I'm shivering already, Charles. Tell me."

"I'm gonna knit you one. I'm gonna do one for you as a payback. That'll sure stop your shivering."

"I can't wait, Charles," said Ms. Mason-Dixon.

"You'd have to promise to wear it all the time."

"No sweat, Charles," said Ms. Mason-Dixon. "Well, let's say no sweat-er!" and she gave that sort of bark she thinks is a laugh. I joined in. You've got to help old people along when they try to crack a joke.

Then she got down to final instructions. Out came two bits of paper. One big oblong and one small oblong. "Knit two bits this size and then two bits that size," she pointed. "Get it? This is your pattern."

"Why two of each?"

"I have a funny feeling, Charles, that the baby your poor mother is carrying will have a back and a front and also two arms. That's if you're anything to go by."

"Yeah. Reckon you could be right. Two of each, eh?"

"Two of each. Whatever colors you like. It doesn't matter. Make it nice and bright. It'll help hide the mistakes. Wash your hands before you start knitting — you don't want to give the baby germs, do you? Poor little mite," said Ms. Mason-Dixon.

"Then what?"

"Bring the four lots back to me and we'll have a go at sewing them up . . . and . . ."

"What, Ms. Mason-Dixon?"

"Best of luck, Charles." She shot out a hand to shake mine.

Spikey and Jacko now call me a greaser. They've been counting up my visits to Ms. Mason-Dixon. They've been spying on me. "I been doing her garden," I told them. "She pays me to do it."

"You haven't done much," said Jacko. "It's still all grown up like a wild jungle."

"I'm digging out the weeds for her from under all the wild jungle," I said.

"Greaser," said Spikey. "Bet you're tryin' to grease your way back onto our team."

Be a bit hard. Alice Pepper used two more words and my knitting friend, Ms. Mason-Dixon, thought it was me and I've been laid off for another two weeks.

"She dumps you off the team just about forever and then you go and do her garden?" Jacko sounded puzzled.

"He's thick," said Alice Pepper, passing by. "That's why. Ms. Mason-Dixon's his grandma's best friend and I reckon that stinks."

"Why?" I asked.

" 'Coz you're her pet. Your grandma pays Ms. Mason-Dixon to make you her pet."

"Well, she can't be paying enough, can she?" I said.

"Why?"

"If I was her pet she wouldn't keep me sitting next to you, Alice Pepper. If I was her pet she wouldn't kick me off our team all the time when *you* swear and she'd give me good marks and she never does."

"Greaser," said Spikey.

"Greaser," said Jacko.

"Teacher's pet," said Alice Pepper.

"Four o'clock sharp, Charles," said Ms. Mason-Dixon. "Lawns. Need I say more? Now, get on with your work, the lot of you."

8

It's very hard to knit in secret round our place. The best place is the loo because that's one room Alice Pepper can't see in. I've done ten rows in the loo and changed from purple to green all by myself. The trouble is, no sooner do I start in on a good knit than Mum's bashing on the door. "Come on, Chas. Please! Chas, I'm bursting."

Mum's going through a bit of her pregnancy when she has to go to the loo a lot because the fetus is pressing on her bladder. I can hardly tell her to go outside because I'm knitting the fetus a sweater.

Knitting in the bath is not easy. I lost a day, and quite a few of my stitches, when I had to dry out the first oblong, and the purple has lost a bit of its color into the green.

Knitting in bed after Dad's put the light out is even harder. I've only got three-quarters of a wall on one side of me because of Dad not finishing it and they'd sure see if I turned the light back on. I've done one-and-a-half rows under my blankets but it's not easy to hold the flashlight and knit. It can be done if you put the flashlight between your knees and pointing up but you've got to hold it very still and it does get a bit hot.

I'll get there.

"Bet you can't even knit yet," said Alice Pepper.

"That's for me to know and you not to find out," I said.

"Five bucks a week for life. You know what? I lay in my bed at night and just dream what I'm gonna do with it all," said Alice Pepper.

Dream on, Alice Pepper. Dream on. Mind you, my first oblong is only as long as my little finger and it has been a week. I think I'll check with Mum and see if she thinks there's a chance of her having a very tiny wee baby — like about the size of my hand! "How's your treehouse going, Pepper?"

"None of your business and it's not part of our bet, not at all. So there!"

"Dad wants that wood back you nicked."

"No he doesn't 'coz I asked him," said Alice Pepper. "And if he did, I'd just go to the cops and tell them he nicked it all in the first place. I've got him over a barrel and he'd go to jail."

I don't think she would go to the cops because Alice Pepper's in love with my dad. So's her mum. Alice Pepper told me that if my mum died she'd marry my dad to make up for it and the only thing stopping her is that she'd end up as my stepmother. You sure would be a wicked stepmother, Alice Pepper! And Mrs. Pepper would be my stepgrandma and that'd be even more wicked!

Mrs. Pepper reckons my dad is dead sexy and it should be him in the ads and not Mum, who's ugly. "My mum says with his long black curly hair and his tight shorts he always wears and nothing else and the kangaroo-skin hat your grandma bought him in Australia, he'd make a fortune doing underpants on the telly because he's so sexy. Mum says she'd sure buy them," Alice Pepper told me.

"What's your mum want men's jockeys for?" I asked her.

"Poor Maureen," said Mum when I told her. "I must have her over for a cup of tea."

For the next week after I told them, Dad spent a lot of time out in our backyard wearing his old shorts and his kangaroo-skin hat. Then we had a cold spell.

I'm not getting far with Munro as a name. Mind you, I don't think Dad's winning with Jo, either. Mum's changed from Alexandra. I think the spelling thing's worried her. For two minutes she thought about Matilda. Matilda is Grandma's name. Dad changed her mind for her. "Over my dead body," said Dad. This is one of his favorite sayings.

"I'm sure Mum will be pleased to arrange that for you, dear," said my mum, very sweetly.

I just think it's funny that all the names Mum

comes up with are girls' names. "You know something, I reckon," I said to her. "You know it's a girl already. Alice Pepper says they know how to tell the sex. She says they poke something up like a telescope and have a look."

"Rubbish," said Mum. "And I don't know. Yes, they can tell but I don't want to know. *We* don't want to know, do we dear?" she said and she took Dad's hand. "It's going to be a big surprise and we're all going to have to wait another ten weeks. If you're very, very good you can have a look at it next week."

"How?" Maybe Alice Pepper was right.

"I'm having a scan next week. They use sound waves to build up a picture and it gets recorded on a screen. I'm going to get a video of it and then we can all watch. It's sort of a check to make sure everything is as it should be." Mum held up a hand. "No, you won't be able to tell its sex. However, we'll all get to have a look, a first look at little Susan."

Susan! It better not be a boy!!

Ten weeks to go.

I've been on the knitting for over two weeks and I'm not even half up (or down) my first oblong.

I got away to the loo and kept my fingers crossed Mum's bladder would hold out for a decent time.

9

I found Mum all alone, sitting on the sofa and having a cry. She tried to hide it. "Goodness," she said. "You're home early. What've you done with Jacko and Spikey?" She looked over my shoulder.

"They gone for haircuts," I said.

"Yes, and you need one, too."

"No, I don't. What's the matter?"

Mum wiped her eyes with the back of her hand and went to put a bright smile on her face but her tears wouldn't stop. "Oh, me? I'm just being silly," she said, and stood up and rubbed her back. "Nothing's the matter," she said, but she didn't stop crying.

I looked at her. "You're sick of having this baby, eh?"

She looked at me and she was sort of crying and laughing. "Yes, you little demon. You got it in one. I'm sick of being as big as a house and my belly's too big and my boobs are too big and getting bigger and I can't see my feet when I stand up and look down. I've got no clothes to wear that are big enough and I don't want to waste any money getting any more."

"Come here." I tried to say it like I heard Dad say it. I didn't wait for her to come to me. I just walked up to her and gave her a big hug. Boy, was it hard! I don't think I got my arms halfway round her middle and my head sort of ended up resting on her big belly. But I did my best. "Now I'll give you a back rub," I said. "Get down on that sofa again. Come on. Do what you're told."

"My word. We have been taking lessons from our father, haven't we? Ah, my little man," she said and she ruffled my hair. "It does need a cut." She kissed me.

My mum. She's not too bad, really, as far as mums go. I don't think I'll trade her in for another one just yet. I made us both a cup of coffee and gave her back a good long rub.

"Better now?" I asked her.

"Heaps better. Might be an idea if you cut your fingernails, love. Don't think you've left too many claw marks. But it sure was a great back rub."

"No more tears." I pointed a finger.

She looked at me as if she might be working up for another go. "Not if you say so," and she sort of rolled over and swung her legs round and finally sat up. She really did look like a small hippopotamus trying to do the same thing. "Just a bit too tired and a bit too big and a bit too silly. Come and sit by me." I got another hair ruffle from her. "You don't mind about the baby, do you?"

"Course not," I almost told the truth. "It's neat, and I'm gonna have a brother and we're gonna call him Munro."

She wasn't biting today. "It's just sort of, well, it's just been the three of us for just about forever and now it's not going to be. Just you'n me and Daddy for over nine years and it's almost, looking back, as if we were all just little kids back then."

"I was the little kid, Mum. You weren't. You were grown up," I said.

"We thought we were," she said and she laughed. "Him'n me? Daddy and me? We were nineteen."

Seemed quite grown up to me. I didn't say anything.

"Thought we knew it all. Goodness knows, if it hadn't been for Grandma . . . are you sure you don't mind?"

It did seem to be just a wee bit late to check whether I minded. I didn't like to say so. "No, of course I don't mind. I'll be your baby-sitter when you want to go out and you can pay me. I'll even take him to hockey with me." That's if I ever got to play again!

"Put your hand there," said Mum. "You can feel the baby moving. See?" She took my hand. "That's my baby." She smiled. "Our baby. Feel it?" She moved my hand about a bit.

I did feel it. Boy, was that spooky. Just under Mum's clothes and through her skin and moving about in all the stuff a baby moves about in was someone I'd never met or seen. Very soon I was going to meet that someone and know them and talk to them and do things with them for the rest of my life. My brother, Munro!

"Drag me to my feet, Charlie boy. I want to get on with dinner before Daddy comes in. I just don't think I could eat another one of his fry-ups, bless him. Not today. And if you tell him I said so, I'll scalp you — and that'll sure take care of the haircut you're going to have tomorrow."

I've found a place under the house for knitting. Won't be able to use it for too long because you crawl to it through the no-floor room that was Mr. Magoo's. Judging by the look of it I think Mr. Magoo must have used it to get away from us all. There were still a few bits of dead birds and an old shirt of Dad's that Mr. Magoo used for sleeping on.

It was under here that I finished the first oblong. It is really beautiful. The mixed-in purple and green looks quite good and then there's a big band of bright, bright pink, one row of gold, and then a nice deep black up to near the top. I've finished it off with a soft white wool because it is for a baby and they have tender skin in places like round the neck.

There is a slight problem. It's not really an oblong

at all. It's a sort of a flower pot shape. I think this might be because I ended up with twenty-seven more stitches up at the top than I had when I started. Well, I reckon it can just have floppy shoulders. Either that or I'll sew it all straight down the side.

I'm going to do a sleeve next because it's quicker. Then I'll know I'm getting somewhere.

Eat yer heart out, Alice Pepper. Those skulls will soon be mine!

10

Ms. Mason-Dixon has given up and I'm back on our team. I think she worked out we'd never win another game without me. Our team has been on a losing streak since Ms. Mason-Dixon booted me out for Alice Pepper's swearing and serves them right. Now, they need my skills.

Even though I shouldn't say so myself I am a master of the hockey stick. I have worked out quite a few tricks of the trade to keep us on the path to victory. It is sad for our team that Ms. Mason-Dixon won't let me use many of my tricks of the trade. She's pretty dead set against using anything that'll traumatize the other side other than our sheer skill and speed. This is a pity because, quite often, we play other sides who need a bit of good, old-fashioned, honest traumatizing. Still, she's the boss.

I think it's going to take me a while to get back into the feel of a hockey stick after the feel of knitting needles all the time. The skills needed for knitting and the skills needed for hockey are not quite the same. Of course, if they were, you'd really need to use two hockey sticks at the same time.

Alice Pepper is off the hockey team. At long long long last Ms. Mason-Dixon got her hearing and ears on the right track and caught Alice Pepper right at it and in the middle of a quiet bit of our human relationships study. Alice Pepper was telling Spikey what he could do with his human relationships and where he could shove his project. Spikey is the big winner. He is now acting captain of our team and Alice Pepper is out for two weeks. About time!

Not only did Alice Pepper end up off the team but she was put out of our classroom. She is now in a clear lead on put-outs — she's had nineteen this year. One more, Ms. Mason-Dixon says, and Alice Pepper gets the big one. We don't know what the big one is because no one's ever won it before. We're all looking forward to finding out.

Put-outs are when you, your desk, and your chair all end up outside the classroom in the corridor. There's no nonsense about it. Ms. Mason-Dixon simply picks you up on your chair, plonks you and your chair on top of your desk, and carries the whole lot out of the classroom while the door monitor holds the door open. I think this is why Ms. Mason-Dixon needs regular workouts at Grandma's gym. She sure is fit is Ms. Mason-Dixon. Alice Pepper is the only one of us who argues with Ms. Mason-Dixon during a put-out. Often their conversations are still going on when Alice Pepper is out in the corridor and Ms. Mason-Dixon is back to math or spelling or human relationships.

Alice Pepper has had nineteen put-outs. I come second. I've had seven. Spikey's had six. Jacko's had one because he's cunning, and one or two others have had three or four.

Spikey reckons the big one for Alice Pepper is probably going to be capital punishment from Mrs. Florence Allan, our principal, even though it's against the law. Mrs. Florence Allan is a lady we don't see very often because of the paperwork. Whatever the big one is, we all want to be around to see it and enjoy it when the axe falls. Kids are now coming to school when they're sick as dogs just so's not to miss out on Alice Pepper's big one. Alice Pepper has been on nineteen for nearly two weeks. I think she's worried.

"She can't do nothing to me," Alice Pepper told me.

"Yes she can," I said. "She can do heaps."

"Like what?"

"Like torture," I said.

"I don't care," she said.

"Yes you do."

"No I don't."

"Yes you do."

"No I don't."

"I know you do," I said. "You're damn worried underneath. I can tell."

"I'm not so. How can you tell?"

I looked at her with a sly look. "Because you haven't had a put-out for nearly two weeks. Most of the time you get one a week. Sometimes you get more'n that," I said. "You're scared, all right. You're dead scared of what's going to happen to you."

"I'm not scared of old Mason-Dixon."

"I bet you're scared of Mrs. Florence Allan."

"Her!!" Alice Pepper said three rude words. "What can she do to me?"

I shook my head. "A lot of things. That's what. You're scared all right."

"Bull!" said Alice Pepper.

It would have been nice to have hung around a bit longer to scare Alice Pepper even more, but I had to get back to my knitting.

I'm coming up to the end of sleeve number one and it looks lovely. It's all in blues and I've done it from pale blue up to navy blue and it's just like a beautiful clear summer sky. I've sorted through my balls of wool and the other sleeve is going to be in greens with maybe a touch of orange or purple because I haven't got as many greens as blues. Orange and green go nice together and the purple will be a good highlight. This sweater is going to be a designer knit. A designer knit is a work of great art. I know this because I heard Mum and Mrs. Maureen Pepper talking about them while Mrs. Pepper was having a cup of tea and giving

Mum a back rub. Designer knits are artistic cloth-ing.

The old flower pot problem is still with me but I've worked out what to do about it. Every few rows I have a count up just to see how many more stitches I've made. Then it's easy. I just pick a good place and knit a few stitches together. It's cool because you then get quite a nice bobbly effect.

Munro is sure going to have one choice sweater. I've got a good mind to do one for myself after I've done his and after I've done one for Ms. Mason-Dixon as a payback for all her good work with me. One thing I know for sure is there'd be nothing else around quite like my designer knits.

11

The doctor has said our baby could come sooner rather than later and I've started knitting faster.

I hope it doesn't come sooner because Dad hasn't put the floor in Mr. Magoo's room yet. He's been far too busy with Ms. Mason-Dixon.

"Boy, that old girl hasn't changed since the days when she used to whack my fingers with the edge of a ruler twenty years ago," he said to Mum. "Whenever she picks up a bit of wood I sort of just freeze all over and I know I won't be able to spell the word she asks me. Then I just wait for that ruler to fall. Ouch!" he said and he pretended it had.

"Yes, dear," said Mum. "You sure couldn't spell back then. I don't think you're any better now, dear."

"Yeah," said Dad. "It's all because of old Dixon."

"If you say so, dear. Not that you ever tried very hard. Twenty years ago, that is."

"Too much else on my mind." Dad grinned.

"Yes, dear. Like teasing the life out of me, if I

remember rightly." Mum grinned back at Dad. "And just look at where it got me." She patted her tummy and looked all around at our comfy mess.

"Yeah," said Dad. "Just about heaven, isn't it?" and he gave her a big kiss.

"If you say so, dear," she said and she kissed him back.

"D'you know, old Dixon even comes home at lunchtime to check on me. She caught me smoking."

"Did she whack you, dear?" asked Mum. "Like it would be a good idea if she did. If anyone could get you to stop smoking it'd be Miss Dixon."

"I think the thought crossed her mind," said Dad. "She sent me to stand outside. I mean right outside. Not even in her garden. She made me stand outside her front gate. D'you know what?"

"What?" asked Mum.

"It felt just the same as when she used to give us put-outs in the corridor and lifted us out, desk, chair, body and all," said Dad.

"You never told me, Dad . . . you never . . . you never ever said you got put-outs in the corridor in the olden days. Dad! You never did. Did you?"

"I think it was only just once," said Dad.

"Liar," said Mum.

"How many did you get, Dad? Come on, Dad. How many? Dad, please! How many did you get?"

"I might've got up to two in one whole year," said Dad.

"Liar," said Mum.

"You got some, too, Liz," said Dad.

"How many, Mum?" Whew! Was this awesome?

"And you tell the truth," said Dad.

"Why? You don't," Mum laughed. "If you must know, Chas, I think I got up to seven."

"MUM!!" Whew!!! Wow, she must've been a bad one. Like, I'm up to seven! And Ms. Mason-Dixon said that Alice Pepper is the only girl, ever, to get up above that.

"Well, she was really tough back then. And don't look at me like that, you little devil. Just you ask your father how many he got," said Mum.

"Dad?"

"Twenty," said Dad, and looked down at the floor making like he was a naughty little boy.

HOT DOUBLE DAMN!!!!!

"So you got the big one, eh?"

"Sure did, Chas," he said quietly and shaking his head.

"What was it, Dad? You can tell me."

"Can't, son. Can't do that. I was sworn to secrecy." He looked at Mum. "And so was your mother," he added, quickly. "Anyone who's copped the big one never ever talks about it."

"What a load of . . ." began Mum.

"Even to his wife," said Dad loudly. "Not ever!"

It is quite clear to me now that I come from a pretty bad family and it's a wonder I'm as good as I am. I've got a feeling it will be up to me to make sure Munro stays on track. He's sure not going to get a good example set to him by his parents! It's probably no wonder Grandma has ended up the way she is. Her daughter, my mum, Liz, must have been one big handful for the poor old lady. Then, to make it worse, she turned round and married Dad, who must have been an even bigger handful. I am beginning to see Grandma in a new light and to feel sorry for her. This is not easy with my grandma.

Grandma owns the gym down past the shops where Ms. Mason-Dixon, her very good friend, works out, does aerobics, and keeps fit. Grandma is fifty-two-and-a-half and although this is old she doesn't look it. She has long blonde hair tied back and wears tracksuits all the time. She can beat me and Alice Pepper, Jacko, and Spikey in any sort of race. Grandma is the daughter of Great-gran, who is seventy-three-and-three-quarters and who owns a pub on a beach up north. This is my dad's very favorite place to go for holidays and so he can help Great-gran. He often says he'd like to live up there all the time so he'd be on the spot to help her more. Well, she is old and probably could do with a bit more help.

Both Grandma and Great-gran have been a bit careless with husbands. This sometimes worries Dad. Grandma's husband, my grandad, died when Mum was a girl. Grandma says that once was enough and hasn't bothered to get another one.

Great-gran has had three husbands and they're all dead and that's all I know about them.

Nana and Pop are Dad's mum and dad. They are the same age as Great-gran because Dad was the youngest in a large family. Nana and Pop also live at a beach but they don't own a pub. They don't like noise. We go to see them just sometimes because their house is not a house for children and it's not nice for them if I traumatize any of their delicate things.

"You haven't even started to knit yet," said Alice Pepper. "I know you haven't started to knit."

"You don't know nuthin', Pepper."

"Can't wait for my five bucks a week for life," Alice Pepper said, rubbing her hands.

"Can't wait for my skull collection, and you better not try sneaking any of them away and hiding them. I know what's there," I said.

"You can't even knit."

"Can so."

"Can't," Alice Pepper said and made a rude finger sign at me.

"Get stuffed, Alice Pepper. Where's yer treehouse, then? Haven't built it at all, eh?"

"I'm waiting to see the baby isn't born dead. I don't want to waste my time building a treehouse for a croaked baby."

"Well it was still alive this afternoon, Alice Pepper," I told her. "So there!"

"How d'you know? Did you have a look in your mum's womb?"

"I didn't have to," I said. "I listened to its heart beating. From the outside."

"Geez. Really? You reckon she'd let me have a listen?"

"Sure. No sweat. But it'll cost you. Mum's charging a buck a listen and you pay me and you don't tell her 'coz she gets all upset. If you want to see the video of her insides with the baby that she's getting done tomorrow it'll cost you even more. We gotta charge heaps to pay the mortgage and the bank manager. You know that."

"How much?"

"I'll let you know when I've worked it out and you gotta book a seat and don't you ever tell Mum. Don't tell *your* mum, either, and she can't come."

12

I'm going to have to do something about the sweater. It's going to be twenty times too big for our baby. At least! I know because I've seen the video. Mum's had her scan and I've seen the evidence. I guess the baby could grow into the sweater but it would sure take a while — like twenty years!

This is going to be one squidgy, small gray baby. To be very honest and to tell the truth, our baby is going to be a small blob. A small gray blob.

"I told you so," said Alice Pepper. "Sure wasn't worth the two bucks you charged me. Your mum has got big problems and my mum was right. I think your baby's got three arms."

I hadn't thought of this! Maybe I should have waited until after the birth before starting the sweater. At least that way I could've seen exactly what we ended up with.

To give Mum her due, she has tried to make excuses and stand up for the blob. "It's only the eighth month. Still a few weeks to go. The doctor says it's perfect."

Perfect!! I think Mum should change doctors right now before it's too late.

To begin with, the blob is very small. This would've been just right, perfect for me, when I was still an amateur beginner knitter. It's sure not right for me now that I'm fully into the swing of designer knitting. I've done about enough knitting to make the blob six sweaters! It's all well and good for Mum to say it's still got a lot of growing to do. She reckons that growing is all that's got to happen to it between now and popping-out time. If it doesn't grow we're in for very big problems. For one, given the mess in our house, we're bound to lose him.

"Where's the baby, dear?" Dad might ask Mum when he comes in from work and wants to have a look.

"I don't know, darling," Mum would have to say back to him, giving him a kiss. "I think I might've lost him somewhere under the sofa. Can't find him anywhere. Check the vacuum cleaner bag, darling."

"Have you looked in the rubbish bin, love?"

"Not today, sweetie. Have a look for me, there's a dear. He could have rolled into your last night's beer can you left under the coffee table. He was having a swim in the sink when I did the dishes but I was careful about the plughole when I let the water out. I don't think he went down."

"Tell you what, Liz, get the old bird cage out. We haven't needed it since Mr. Magoo croaked Oscar.

If we find the baby this time we'll keep him in there, darling."

I ask you!!!

Of course there is another little problem with our blob. It's a problem of color. Look, I don't mind a black one, a white one, a brown one, or a red or a yellow one. But who in their right mind wants a gray baby? A gray baby? The only good thing about having a gray baby is that my sweater is bound to brighten him up a bit. I know it doesn't matter at all what people look like. Mum and Dad are always telling me this and they're quite right. It is just as well they think this way. I guess we can all put up with small and gray, but I do wonder just how long the three of us can live with what's going to be the ugliest little human being ever created.

The whole thing has been too much for Dad. I found him out in the middle of the backyard. I'm sure he'd worked his way through a whole pack of cigarettes. Poor old Dad. I feel for him.

"Never mind, Dad," I said softly. "Better luck next time, eh? That's if you're brave enough to have another go."

He was so far out of it I don't even think he was listening. "Wonderful, Chas, wasn't it? A bloody miracle!" He shook his head. I think the poor old guy was in a daze.

Poor, poor man. Still, what could I say? After all it was half his and it was only fair he had to take half the blame. "A bloody miracle indeed, Dad." It was my job to help him through this. It must be that miracles aren't always good things.

"Did you see its little arms and legs? Whew!" Dad went on shaking his head.

"Yeah," I said. "He had quite a few of them, eh? Sort of lots of little jerky ones."

"And its little head." The poor man couldn't stop shaking his. "Its little head!"

There was nothing I was going to say about that one!

"To think that I . . ." More head shaking, and then he looked at me. "Wow, Chas! Just think, you were just like that once upon a time. And you know what?"

I shuddered deeply. "No. What?"

"It seems just like yesterday." Dad smiled down on me.

Poor poor poor man. It's all been too much for him. But he needn't worry. Him and Mum have still got me and I'll stand by them in their hour of need. If you're a family you've got to face these things together. That's just what families are all about.

"I think I could see it was a boy," said Alice Pepper. "I'm pretty sure it had something hanging between its legs. That's cool. Looking like that it'd be better off and happier as a boy. I think it looks just like you."

"You couldn't see nuthin', Alice Pepper." I felt low, real low. One part of me wanted to agree with

Alice Pepper. The other part of me had to stand by this baby because it was ours.

"Yeah. He's a boy, all right. I think one of those things that looked like a hand or a foot or a leg or an arm was probably its thingy."

"You can't tell whether it's a boy or a girl," I said.

"Or a monkey," said Alice Pepper. "A monkey'd be right cool."

"Then you better get double busy with your tree-house, then, hadn't you," I said nastily. "It's gonna need it."

Jacko and Spikey have seen the video of Mum's scan. We watched it eleven times after hockey practice. Mum was out doing her last telly ad before the baby comes. She's doing one for the health people on how nice it is to breast-feed your baby and it's cheaper, too. I just hope and pray they don't want to do a follow-up one after she's got the poor little thing. While the camera may work wonders on Mum and turn her from being ugly into a great beauty, I doubt that it'll do much for our baby. Still, if she has to, we could be lucky. It's unlikely the cameras would even spot the tiny wee thing. It'll be lost down there somewhere between her boobs.

I didn't have the heart to charge Spikey and Jacko for seeing the video. Be hard, anyway. They've never got any money.

"How's it breathe in there?" asked Jacko.

"Doesn't," I said. "Doesn't need to till it's born."

"Bit like an astronaut," said Spikey. "It's like your old lady's the mother ship and the kid's got its life-support system with that cord."

"Looks hungry to me," said Jacko. "So'm I. Your old lady got any biscuits?"

"No."

"Your old man got any beer?" asked Spikey.

"No."

"Wonder if it can talk?"

"Babies can't talk. They can't talk even when they're born," I said.

"They can make noises and cry," said Spikey. "Can I have a look in the fridge?"

"What happens when it wants to go to the bathroom?" Jacko asked.

"Dunno," I said. "Probably it doesn't."

"I do," said Spikey, and went.

"They do go to the bathroom," said Jacko. "I asked my old lady once. She says it just gets taken back, absorbed into the mum."

13

The second sleeve is finished. I wonder if I should do a spare one? I've got enough wool. It could be needed and it wouldn't be too hard to fit on.

The second sleeve is lovely. I know I shouldn't say so myself but any knitter would be proud of it. The orange and gold band I've put in the middle just sets off the green so nicely. It's quite a bit longer than the first sleeve but (and I'm thinking of our poor baby on video) I don't really think this matters. This little child is not going to be the sort of little child who has two the same of anything!

The floor is now closed up in Mr. Magoo's room. These days Dad calls it Jo's room. Mum, who's gone back to her first choice, calls it Alex's room. I try to call it Munro's room but I have to admit it's hard. I must be honest — it does seem to be the waste of a perfect name.

The problem of where to knit is forever with me. A snatched couple of rows in the loo won't be enough to see me through the back by B-Day. I've now started knitting in the bath when it hasn't got any water in it. Also, instead of trying it *in* my bed I've found it easier to get down to it *under* my bed. My design for the front (or back) of the sweater is going to be quite excellent. I've worked out how to knit with three balls of wool at the same time. I do ten stitches of one color, ten of another color, and then ten of a third color. Then, when I'm sick of one of those first lots, I just make another change. I've used every color Ms. Mason-Dixon gave me. I'm sure she'll be pleased.

I've also worked out how to make the plain stitch Ms. Mason-Dixon taught me a bit more interesting here and there. My favorite thing to do is to knit two stitches together (or sometimes three if I can stuff the needle through three at the same time) and then make a new stitch altogether. It comes out totally different from just the plain knitting. Yes indeed, this sweater will certainly brighten up one little gray life. With any luck I'm hoping that everyone's eyes will hit on the sweater and not look too hard at what's wearing it.

Alice Pepper nearly got put-out number twenty. I'm pleased to say it was almost all my fault.

"How come, Ms. Mason-Dixon," I began, "you're Ms. Mason-Dixon now and you were only Miss Dixon when you taught my mum and dad in the olden days?" It seemed an interesting question for during science.

"It's none of your business, Charles," she said,

and then she thought she'd change her mind. "Well, maybe it is. Maybe we might find something in there to learn. I must admit I'm getting a little tired of caterpillars."

Well, caterpillars are certainly more interesting than the very long and very boring talk Ms. Mason-Dixon gave us. It was all about women always getting men's names and how unfair and sexist it was. First off they got given their dad's name and then, if they got married (and Ms. Mason-Dixon decided at a young age that this was for the birds and not a good idea for her), they ended up with the name of the man they married unless they were very tough (and Ms. Mason-Dixon would have been very tough if she had made a mistake and got married to some man). So, after all that, she decided to put her mother's name on the front of Dixon. Her mother's name, before she made the mistake of getting married to a man, was Mason.

Alice Pepper made her first mistake. "I think you got tricked, Ms. Mason-Dixon," she said.

"How come, Alice?"

"Well, if your mother's name was Mason before she got married, that would've been her dad's name. See what I mean, Ms. Mason-Dixon? Instead of you ending up with one man's name you've ended up with two of them. That's very sad for you, Ms. Mason-Dixon."

"That's true, Alice, but, you see, it's the . . ."

Alice Pepper did not give Ms. Mason-Dixon a

chance. "So then you'd have to go back to your grandma, and say her name was Fishhead then you would be Ms. Fishhead-Mason-Dixon, but Fishhead would've been her dad's name and you'd have to go back to your great-grandma and if her name was . . ."

"I think we get your point, Alice."

". . . Crocodile, then you'd be Ms. Crocodile-Fishhead-Mason-Dixon and you could go on and on and on forever and have the longest name ever invented in the whole wide world and they'd all belong to old dead men. Geddit? You could get in the Guinness Book of World Records for long names. Good one, eh?"

Ms. Mason-Dixon got Alice Pepper off names with another boring talk about how Mason-Dixon was a famous name in history. "It's the name of the line between the North and the South that chops the United States of America in two."

Alice Pepper got to put-out nineteen-and-a-half when she turned to the whole class and said, "Ms. Mason-Dixon is a lion that chomps America in two."

Sadly I must report that Alice Pepper was saved from the big one by Mrs. Florence Allan, our principal, coming in the door at the wrong time with some papers for Ms. Mason-Dixon. They had a long talk about the papers over the top of Alice Pepper, on her chair, on her desk, while we all crossed our

fingers and held our breaths waiting . . . hoping
. . . waiting . . . hoping . . . but . . .

The bell went.

"Saved by the bell, Alice," said Ms. Mason-Dixon, from one side of Alice Pepper. "Saved by the bell."

"This time," said Mrs. Florence Allan, from the other side of Alice Pepper.

14

It looks like our baby's already here. There are thirty-six brand-new nappies on our clothesline. Mum's washed them all ready for B-Day.

"She should've kept your old nappies and saved some money for the bank manager and the mortgage," said Alice Pepper. "But I suppose you still need yours and she wouldn't want the germs from your piddle to hurt her baby. When are the bank manager and the cops coming to chuck you out?"

"You gotta hole in your head," I said to Alice Pepper.

"I gotta lotta holes in my head, piddle pants," said Alice Pepper. "And don't you start thinking when they chuck you out that you get off my five bucks a week for life. I'll track you down wherever you go. You might have to sleep under a bridge or you could live in your grandma's gym."

Grandma now spends as much time at our place as Alice Pepper usually does. She only goes to her own home when Dad gets back from work. I think the gym must be running itself. She gives Mum

"That's cool," said Dad.

"Oh, she did say to tell you that you're down to just one pair of good jeans," said Mum.

"Hey!" said Dad. "Hold on. I know I've got three or four pairs."

"No longer, dear." And Mum gave him a big kiss to make up for it.

I stood in Mr. Magoo's room. I just wonder what the old boy would've made of it all. Well, he would've made short work of the chickens and ducks on the curtains and that's for sure. I guess he would've slept in the cot and used the carpet as a claw sharpener and litter box. Mr. Magoo was never the world's best house-trained cat.

I wonder if our little gray blob will feel the ghost of Mr. Magoo in this room. I wonder if on dark and windy stormy nights the Mr. Magoo howl will haunt the sleep of little Munro. Probably not. If the video is anything to go by it doesn't look like we're getting a sensitive baby who'd feel these things. It might be just as well for Mr. Magoo that he was traumatized and croaked.

15

What I thought would be the worst thing possible has happened. I've been caught knitting. Not by Mum. Not by Dad. Not by Grandma. Not by Alice Pepper. I've been caught knitting by Jacko and Spikey.

Mum was at the doctor's for what she says will be her last checkup before B-Day. Dad was out chasing another building job now that he's finished Ms. Mason-Dixon's. I told Alice Pepper that Grandma was in our house so I didn't have to worry about her snooping round.

I settled down right out in the open. I sat cross-legged on our kitchen table to do my last finger's worth of knitting on the back (or front) of Munro's sweater. (I measure my knitting in fingers because it seems as good a way as any to do it.)

The knitting was going real good. The needles, the wool, and my fingers all just fly, now, almost so quick you can't see them. I can now do up to seven stitches flat out, nonstop, with my eyes closed before I make a mistake or lose a stitch. It's choice.

The last bit is white-spotted black. I do a few black stitches and then pop in a white one. It looks very good. The bit before I did the opposite. I'd do a few white stitches and then pop in a black one. Both of these lots are above a nice bright yellow, which is on top of a pale blue that matches the chickens on Munro's curtains. Blue chickens? Poor little baby. Just imagine him growing up thinking all chickens are blue and all ducks are green. It's Grandma's fault.

"Watcha doin'?" Spikey pushed in the door.

"An egg truck lost its load and rolled down the hill. C'mon. We're gonna see the scrambled eggs." Jacko pushed past Spikey. "Whatcha doin'?"

They sort of stood there blinking for a minute.

"Knittin'," I said.

"Knittin'," said Spikey.

"Knittin'," said Jacko.

"That's cool," said Spikey.

"Sure cool," said Jacko. "Come'n see the eggs."

"Gotta get me knittin' done," I said.

"Come'n see the eggs and we'll all do yer knittin' when we get back. Where's yer old lady?" asked Spikey.

"Doctor's."

"What's in yer fridge?" Spikey had a look. "You only got veggies now, eh. Once your fridge was real cool. All sorts of junk."

"It's Grandma," I said.

"Where?" They both jumped and looked all about them.

"Grandma makes us eat all the veggies. It's good for our baby."

"How come you eatin' veggies is good for your baby?"

"How come your old man eatin' veggies is good for your baby?"

"Coz, if my old lady sees us both eatin' veggies she'll feel like eatin' some, too, and that'd be good for our baby."

"Poor baby," said Jacko. "I think your old lady should stick to burgers and Coke."

"And fried chicken," said Spikey.

"And biscuits and cakes," said Jacko. "And chips."

"Yeah, an' ice cream. Baby'd like all that stuff. On yer bike, Mike, an' we'll go and see the scrambled-up eggs."

The scrambled eggs were excellent! The eggs were everywhere and no one seemed to know what to do about the broken boxes, all the egg trays, and a whole sea of yellowy goo that was right across a hollow in the road. People were everywhere, too, and some were getting free eggs by slushing around and grabbing in the goo. A cop car had skidded and three other cars had skidded into the cop car. People were yelling and a whole crowd cheered when a guy on a motorbike didn't see the cop who was directing traffic and sprayed him all over with egg goo. Then the guy on the motorbike got stuck. It was better than anything you ever see on the telly.

They say all good things must come to an end and, sadly, that's what happened with the scrambled eggs. Even though nothing was on fire the fire brigade came. Soon everything was cleaned up. Those fire guys sure know their jobs.

"I wanna do some knittin'," said Jacko when we got back to my place. "I'm good at it."

"Me, too," said Spikey. "I like it."

Well well well! What a surprise! If only I had known my best mates (not counting Alice Pepper, and I've gone off her since I found out she's very greedy and only wants me for what she can get out of me) were expert knitters. They could have taught me and saved me from bulk lawn mows and from Ms. Mason-Dixon. Mind you, I bet they wouldn't have given me all the wools and the needles.

"What is it? You knittin' a pot holder for your old lady, Chas?" asked Jacko.

"Nah. You guess," I said. "It's got other bits," I got them out to show them. "They all gotta be joined up together," I explained.

Jacko guessed a bathmat, a wheelbarrow, and a shopping bag.

Spikey guessed a cow (if you stuffed it), two hats, a Christmas tree with the lights on, and a stripy elephant with one leg (if you stuffed it).

They were amazed when I told them what it was. Now I've got to knit four more — one for Ms. Mason-Dixon as a payback, one for me, one for Spikey, and one for Jacko. "You gotta give me the wool," I said, "and I'll do it on those real big needles about as big as a hockey stick so's it doesn't take so long. I reckon Mum and Dad'll want one, too," and this was very true now that most of our clothes were at the dump. "Reckon I'll be knittin' for years."

"I reckon you could do a whole heap for our hockey team, Chas," said Jacko. "Sure beats what old Mason-Dixon makes us wear."

I got out the Bible and made them both swear on it and God would slit their throats if they ever told Alice Pepper, and we had a carrot each for afternoon tea. Then I let them knit two rows each of Munro's sweater. Jacko did two rows in a nice bright red and put in little holes his mum had shown him how to do. Spikey did two rows in a soft green in what he called back-to-front knitting. Then I did two of my black rows with white spots flat out so they could see how good I was.

Half a finger to go. Even less if I stretch it out a bit!

"Any day. That's what she says," said Mum when she got home from the doctor's. "Whew!" she flopped down on the sofa. "Make me a coffee, my love. Any day can't come a moment too soon."

16

"Oh dear me," said Ms. Mason-Dixon.

"My my my," said Ms. Mason-Dixon.

"This calls for a considerable feat of engineering," said Ms. Mason-Dixon.

"Where to from here?" asked Ms. Mason-Dixon, as we sat looking at my four oblongs.

"Where there's a will there's a way," said Ms. Mason-Dixon. "Where there's life there's hope," she added.

"Did you use a tape measure, boy?" inquired Ms. Mason-Dixon.

"You do know what an oblong is? No, don't say anything."

"Oh dear me," Ms. Mason-Dixon started to repeat herself.

I think she was stunned at my great success. It was very very true, looking at my four oblongs, that I had come up with the miracle Ms. Mason-Dixon had told me I needed. Boy, it felt good!

"Right." Ms. Mason-Dixon got down to work. "Here." She shoved a big sewing needle, a ball of wool, and an old sweater of hers into my hands. "You get busy practicing some blanket stitch, and I'll get on with a bit of tucking, pinning, and er . . . well . . . I'll see what I can do."

"I'm not making a blanket, Ms. Mason-Dixon," I reminded her.

"Pity." She gave a big sigh. "It would've been much easier." She looked at me, gave another big sigh, and then set about teaching me how to do blanket stitch. It took her a little while.

"My God! You'll see the poor little devil a mile away," said Ms. Mason-Dixon, back at her pinning and tucking.

"That's good, eh?" I said. "For safety on the road and things."

"I think its arms will drag on the floor," said Ms. Mason-Dixon. "Twice over! Are you sure you used the paper pattern I gave you?"

"Sure as, Ms. Mason-Dixon. Couldn't have done without it," I said.

"What on earth is Matilda going to say? Just don't let on to Gran that I had anything at all to do with this, Charles."

"It'll be our secret, Ms. Mason-Dixon," I said, and stuck myself with the needle and used two bad words quite loudly.

I needn't have worried because almost at the same time Ms. Mason-Dixon said, "Bloody hell!" and I was so amazed I stuck myself again.

I don't think I've ever had a feeling like the feeling I had when we both stood back and looked down on the sweater I had made for Munro all by myself (not counting two rows from Jacko; two rows from Spikey; and the tucking, pinning, and some sewing up from Ms. Mason-Dixon). My designer knitting!!

"It'll sure keep the little brute warm," said Ms. Mason-Dixon. "Indeed I think it might cook it," she added.

"What can I say?" I said, shaking my head at the wonder of it all.

"As little as possible," said Ms. Mason-Dixon. "This calls for a celebration." She got out two wineglasses and a bottle of wine. I was a bit sorry she poured lemonade over the squinty bit she gave me, but it could've been she only had one bottle and she needed the rest for herself. "Cheers," she said, and raised her glass.

"Cheers," I replied.

"Here's to your coat of many colors, Charles, and to whoever gets to wear it." Ms. Mason-Dixon lifted her glass again.

"It's a sweater, Ms. Mason-Dixon. It's not a coat," I said.

"Whatever," she said, pouring more wine into her glass but not into mine.

The little sweater of many colors sat on the table and I wondered just who would wear it. Oh, it looked just so great.

"A gift such as this needs a good wrapping," said

Ms. Mason-Dixon. "Here. I knew I'd find a use for this old rubbish." And she took out of a cupboard a box made of silver paper, a mountain of white tissue paper, and a long yellow ribbon. It all looked brand new to me. She helped me to wrap and pack the sweater and tie the yellow ribbon in a big bow around the box.

"Thank you, Ms. Mason-Dixon," I said, as she showed me out of her house. "Thank you for everything. I am really and truly grateful."

"Little greaser," she said. "Get out."

I turned at her front gate to give her a wave. She was still standing there, a little smile on her old face and wiping her eyes. "I couldn't have done it without you, Ms. Mason-Dixon," I yelled, and then waved.

"Make it five more lawn mows, Charles," she called. "Then we're quits."

"Bull," I said under my breath, and ran home. It was time to start moving everything around in my bedroom to make room for my skull collection.

Got you this time, Alice Pepper!

17

D_{r.} Patel has told Mum she'd rather Mum had our baby in hospital than at home.

Mum has told Dr. Patel that she's going to have our baby at home and that pregnant women are not sick women. Besides, she says, not only will she have Dr. Patel to help but she'll have Mrs. White, the midwife. A midwife is a nurse whose special job is delivering babies.

Grandma has told Mum very many times that if she had her way she'd cart Mum off to the hospital to have our baby and tie her down until it came and knock her out while it was coming.

Mum has told Grandma that she's already had one that way and once was quite enough.

Mrs. Maureen Pepper has told Alice Pepper who has told Mum that if there are complications our baby'll croak and older women should be more responsible towards their little babies.

Mum has told Alice Pepper (who has probably told Mrs. Maureen Pepper) that along with the other fifty thousand babies or so who are born into this world every day, hers will have to take its chances of croaking along with the rest and it's got no more chance of doing it at home than in hospital.

Dad has told Mum to do what she likes because that's what she's always done and why change the habits of a lifetime. Dad wants to be in charge of boiling up the water like they do in old movies on the telly when a baby's getting popped out. He wants to find out what they use all the boiling water for and he hopes it's not for cooking up the baby.

Mum has told Dad she can always rely on him for a sensible comment or suggestion.

I have told Mum I'm going to watch the whole thing and with all her contacts can she get a cameraman to film it or video it. I know Alice Pepper, Spikey, and Jacko are interested and will pay heaps to see it. I could ask Ms. Mason-Dixon if we could show the whole class. Or ask Mrs. Florence Allan and we could show the whole school. It'd be very good for all of them to see it and at two bucks each we'd make quite a bit for the bank manager and the mortgage.

Mum has told me I'm very welcome to be there when our baby pops out. She has said no to the film or video idea. I find this disappointing in someone who is so often in front of a camera and who looks ten times better in pictures and stuff than in real life.

* * *

Dad's still going for Jo.

Mum's off Alexandra, has not gone back to Susan, but is on to Victoria.

I still have hopes for Munro. I have to admit they are dim hopes. The choice and the decision seems to be out of my hands. It doesn't matter anyway. I have decided I'm going to call our baby Munro and no one can stop me. I just know that he'll like it. He'd sure like it better than Victoria if he's my kind of guy! Of course he will be my kind of guy because we come from the same mum and dad.

"It's a pity," said Alice Pepper. "You'll never really know your little sister."

"Of course I will."

"No you won't."

"Yes I will."

"No you won't. When she's just little you'll be about nineteen. You don't see many nineteen-year-old guys getting round with little girls. I don't, anyway."

"We won't be getting round," I said.

"No you won't. And when she's still only young you'll be old like your mum and dad and she'll still be having a good time with surfies."

"I could still have a good time then. I think," I said.

"She won't have anything to do with you until she's ninety and you're ninety-nine. Even then she'll find it hard. Specially if you've croaked and you will be by then," said Alice Pepper.

"How's your skull collection, Alice Pepper?" I asked. "Had a last look at it? Don't you forget I want them all dusted and polished."

"You haven't knitted anything. I know that. You couldn't have knitted anything or I'd know." She sounded, I thought, just a tiny wee wee bit doubtful and worried. "You can't knit and when could you have done it and I didn't see?"

"That's for me to know and you to find out, Pepper," I said, smiling nicely.

"And even if you have, I bet it wasn't you did it. I bet you might've got your grandma to do it for you. I'll know if you have," she said.

"You don't know nuthin', Alice Pepper. You're just gonna have to wait and see and eat yer heart out and polish up my skull collection."

Spikey and Jacko are giving me lessons on how to be a brother.

"You gotta start as you mean to go on," said Spikey. "No nonsense. You gotta get 'em working for you and it's very good for them."

"Not it's not," said Jacko. "Mine've got me working all the time except when I can escape."

"You gotta teach 'em if they got money they gotta share it. That's good for them, too, and it stops them being selfish," said Spikey.

"Mine just take my money," said Jacko. "Sometimes they give me a bit back."

"You gotta teach them to keep out of your stuff and out of your room. I want my old man to let me get an electric-shock doorknob. That'd be choice to keep 'em out of my room."

"Yeah," said Jacko. "You gotta be ready to let 'em take all your very own stuff. Then they call it their own."

"You got it made, Chas, what with your one going to be so little," said Spikey.

"You sure have," said Jacko, with a bit of a sad sound in his voice.

18

It's driving Dad and me out of our minds! Mum's gone mad!! All the bits of our house that Grandma hadn't cleaned and tidied, Mum's tackled head-on. We can't stop her. She's even done again some of the bits Grandma did. Now she's borrowed Grandma's pickup and three more loads of our stuff have gone to the dump. Dad says he's down to having less than no pairs of jeans and at this rate he'll soon be walking round with nothing on. He says there is no need for us to worry about paying the mortgage because soon we won't have any house left. I've told him to stop worrying and why don't we all just move out to the dump. We'd feel more at home out there with all our stuff around us than in our nearly empty house.

Mum didn't stop cleaning until Dad walked slap bang into the glass door that goes outside from the lounge. He half knocked himself out. Usually it's very hard to see through our glass doors, but this one was so clean Dad didn't even spot it was there!

* * *

Our baby started popping out at five o'clock in the morning. By the time I got woken up by all the noise it was after seven. I wasn't too late because the best part was still to come.

Dad and Dr. Patel and Mrs. White, the midwife, were with Mum.

"You OK, Mum?" I asked.

"Cool as, Chas," said Mum, with a little smile. "Wow! That was a big one. Get him some breakfast, Jim."

"There's no need for me here," said Dr. Patel. "Give me a call in an hour or so," she said to Mrs. White. "Or if you need me. Don't think you will."

Dad and me had toast and tea and he filled me in on what had happened so far. Just after five in the morning Mum's waters had broken, and now the baby's head was engaged and it was starting its journey out of Mum. Just a matter of time. It could take a long time. It could take a little time. Dad hoped it would take a little time. Mind you, and I've got to say this, I think Mum looked better than Dad! I told him I didn't mind if he had a quick cigarette and Mum wouldn't know if he opened all the windows. It seemed a good time to remind him about the biggest, fattest, and richest cigar we would soon be sharing.

A loud yelp from Mum took us back into the bedroom in double-quick time. Dad put one of his arms around her and clung tight to one of her hands as she knelt, leaning forward. I held her other arm real tight and I know we both, Dad and me, tried to help her as she pushed down hard. She pushed and pushed and pushed. She moaned sort of softly and without stopping for some time as Mrs. White just sort of calmly and quietly talked her through things. Sometimes all you could hear was all of us just breathing and then Mum'd call out for a bit. To be very honest Mum said quite a few words she shouldn't have said. This is quite understandable. Labor is hard work.

"It's coming . . . it's coming . . ." said Mrs. White. "Harder dear, just one more go. Push, now . . ."

At nineteen minutes past eight in the morning our baby was born. It really did just pop out and I saw it all. Curly wet black hair first of all, and then a tiny tiny tiny wee squashed-up face and a flat nose, all a bit gooey and messy. Coming quicker, quicker and on down to the astronaut cord and its funny little arms (just two of them) and finally its little legs (just two of them) and Mrs. White caught the baby and said, as she held it, "Ten fingers, ten toes, nice and neat between the legs and you've got yourself a fine healthy baby daughter with a good strong pair of lungs."

My sister was making the first yell of her life as Dad cut the cord that had joined her to Mum and then Mrs. White handed her to Mum to hold and to feel while she waited for the afterbirth bits and pieces to do their popping out.

Mum was crying and laughing and smiling all

at once. Dad was crying and laughing and smiling all at once and wiping Mum's face with a cloth. It's a great wonder that my very small sister was not traumatized completely as the four of us enjoyed one great big giant and very wet hug!

I didn't have to go to school that day.

19

What a day!

The only time the phone seemed to stop ringing was when Mum or Dad were on it. There were soon a lot of flowers everywhere, and I seemed to spend most of my time making cups of coffee. After lunch Mum got up for a while.

Mum took one look at herself in the mirror and said, "Holy cow!" very loudly and went to have a shower. To tell the truth she sure didn't look much like she does on the telly ads — but then she never really does in real life. For one thing she still looked pregnant. For another thing she did look pretty tired and worn out. I suppose I would be, too, if I had a baby, and that's a miracle that's never likely to happen.

Dad had a snooze for a while. When he wasn't snoozing or on the phone he just lay about doing nothing and with a big grin on his face. I'd have to keep an ear and eye out to make sure I warned him when Grandma arrived. He kept on shaking his head and saying things like, "One of each, now.

One of each. Bloody wonderful!" and then doing some more smiling. So far there was no sign of the cigar but I guess it was still early in the day.

The smile came off Dad's face triple quick when Mum got him to change my sister's first nappy. "Fair's fair," said Mum. "I'll feed her, dear. You just clean up after the feeds."

"I think I'd rather have it the other way around," said Dad.

"No way," said Mum, "I've got a feeling us girls are going to have to stick together," and she started nursing our baby just to prove it.

Just how did this tiny tiny tiny baby know how to suck? How does any baby know? Well, I suppose that's a real miracle, all right.

The only one of the four of us who did not seem at all excited about anything was our baby. Mind you, I suppose she could just have been a bit tired, too, after all her struggles and work to get out of Mum. So far she hasn't even cried much. Just eats and sleeps. Oh, she wets and poos, too. She's a very normal baby.

Mrs. White's coming back later to help Mum give our baby her first bath. After that Grandma's coming. I don't know why she's bothering because she's on the phone every ten minutes and our baby isn't that much to look at and Grandma's bound to be disappointed. Still, she is her only granddaughter. Mind you, I'm Grandma's only grandson and she's not all that keen on me! Nana and Pop are waiting till the weekend to come and have their look. They are going to stay with Grandma because there'll be less noise there.

I've unwrapped and wrapped up again my sweater for my baby sister five times. The tissue paper and the yellow ribbon now look quite old. I'm going to give the sweater to my sister after her first bath.

There is a small problem. Well, maybe a big problem, really. It is a great relief to me that our baby is certainly not the blob I thought she would be. She looks nothing like her video. Unlike our mum, our baby is better in real life than on film. She is not gray. She is a sort of cream color with a touch of pink and she has a great big mop of spiky black hair. Mum thinks she'll end up with brown eyes but it's too soon to tell. No, the problem is not the baby. The problem is the sweater. My sweater would take three or four of our baby and there'd still be room for them to play a game in it. On the one hand this is a pity. This kid looks the sort of kid who'd love to jump straight into a sweater like mine. On the other hand it's probably good she'll have to wait a while to do the jumping because then she'll have something to look forward to in life and this is very important. I think my baby sister might be quite old before she gets to jump into her sweater.

*   *   *

Mrs. White, the midwife, has been and done her stuff and gone. She's so pleased with our baby you'd think she'd had it herself.

Dr. Patel has been and gone. She's as pleased as Mrs. White. "Must admit, Liz, she looks more like me than you," said Dr. Patel.

"Hey," said Dad. "I did have something to do with it. This baby's the spittin' image of me."

"Poor kid," laughed Dr. Patel. "What are you going to call her?" she asked, as Dad refilled her glass of bubbly.

"Still deciding," Mum said to Dad. "Aren't we, dear?"

Mum was feeding the baby and Dad was pretending to help her when Grandma arrived. I was looking out the window and feeling a bit out of things when I saw Grandma's truck pull into our drive. I sighed.

Grandma jumped out of her truck and dragged out boxes and flowers and dumped them on the front doorstep. Then she went back to her truck and got a small box off the front seat. She didn't know I was watching her.

At the front door she opened up the box and lifted out of it one of the smallest, ugliest kittens you've ever seen. She put it right at the front door and held up a warning finger to it not to move. Well, with Grandma around nothing's going to move if she holds up her finger. Then she caught sight of me spying on her. "Ssshhh . . ." she seemed to whisper to me, finger to her lips. Then she winked at me and gave me a big wide grin. I winked back at her. Grandma then picked up all the boxes and flowers and made off round the house and came in by the back door.

"Right! What's going down round here? Don't tell me you've got another baby, Elizabeth? Surely one was enough," she said just as if she never knew. Then there were hugs and laughs and tears and once again the baby was lucky not to be traumatized.

"Good Lord! What on earth's that squawking sound I can hear outside?" said Grandma, walking over to the window. "Don't tell me . . . yes . . . dear God! You've gone and got yourself another cat. Now I've seen everything."

"Eh?" said Dad.

"Yep," I said. "It's a cat, Dad. It's right by the front door. It's a kitten and it looks . . . it looks just like. . . ."

"Mr. Magoo Two," breathed Dad, shaking his head.

"For heaven's sake, Charles, pop the damn thing in the truck for me, boy. I'll drop it in at the vet's to get put down," said Grandma.

"Not on your life, Matilda," said Dad. "No way." He was still shaking his head. "It's . . . it's . . . it's uncanny. . . ."

There are some times when my father is not only as thick as a brick, he's thicker than a mountain of bricks!

20

Grandma bent one of her many lifetime rules and went out and bought us pizzas. She took most of the things that make a pizza a pizza off Mum's slices and made Mum drink a glass of fresh carrot juice and then a glass of milk. I did notice that Grandma enjoyed eating all the bits and pieces she'd taken off Mum's pizza while she and Dad got going on quite a few glasses of bubbly.

Our baby had Mum's milk for dinner and then went back to her cot for a sleep.

Mr. Magoo Two had cow's milk for dinner and went back to the hot-water cupboard for a sleep.

"No no no! Not that dreadful child, please," said Grandma as she watched Alice Pepper walk up to our house. "She sounds like the Three Billy Goats Gruff and looks like the troll from under their bridge."

"I've come to see the baby and Mum says she's heard it howling already and don't forget you promised me a cigar," Alice Pepper said to Dad. "I knew it'd be a girl. Gee, you're sure lucky to get a girl.

You wouldn't want another one like him!" she pointed. "You can always tell, Mum says."

"I don't know how," said Grandma.

"Mum's coming over tomorrow to check it's all right," said Alice Pepper. "It's not deformed, is it?"

"Come on, Alice," said Mum from the sofa. "We'll go and check. I couldn't do without your opinion and I just hope and pray she comes up to your high standards and I've not let the side down."

"I'm sure you done your best, Mrs. Kenny," said Alice politely. "Where is it?"

So we all gathered around our baby yet again. The little dot didn't seem to mind all the looking at she was getting. I suppose this is what you would expect from the daughter of someone who's always had a love affair with the camera.

"She's got the right sort of hands for hockey," said Alice Pepper. "They're big already. Better'n Charlie's, not that that'd be hard. What's that peg thing stuck on her navel for?" she asked.

"If she cries we just peg her up out on the clothesline," said Dad.

"Don't listen to him, Alice," said Mum. "It's just until the last bit of her cord drops off. It takes a few days."

"This baby's sure brought me good luck," said Alice Pepper, smiling.

"How do you work that out, Alice?" asked

Grandma. "You're not having one, too, are you? Nothing would surprise me."

"Ask him what I mean." Alice Pepper pointed at me.

I knew exactly what Alice Pepper meant. "Hang on," I said. "Hang on just a minute," and I went to get my present for my sister.

"Ye Gods and little fishes!" said Grandma. "What's that?"

"Ch . . . Ch . . . Ch . . . Ch . . . Chas," said Mum, and burst into tears as she held the sweater.

"Every stitch a stitch of love, eh man?" said Dad, putting one arm around Mum and one arm around me. "It's . . . it's beautiful, son. Sure is a wondrous work of art." He took the sweater from Mum.

"You'd never get another one like it," said Grandma. "Not anywhere," and she put an arm around me and gave me an enormous hug. Being as fit as she is, Grandma isn't easy to get away from and her hug was a bit like a hammerlock round my neck.

Give Alice Pepper her due, she's not a bad loser in a bet. After a few private words with me, any of which would have got her put-out number twenty, she took off home to start polishing up her skull collection. My skull collection! I'm hoping to add to it quite soon and I have decided to share it with my sister and to let Alice Pepper look at it whenever she likes.

* * *

"Well," said Grandma. "I'll just have my last little look for today at my granddaughter. Is it still to be Alexandra?" she looked at Mum. "I'd best let your grandmother know, Elizabeth, when I phone her."

"Oh no, Mum. I've changed my mind," said my mum. "I still like Alex as a name. Maybe I'll keep it for our next one."

"There'll be no next one, Elizabeth," said Grandma, firmly.

"I've not heard any of this," said Dad. "Don't you think we should sort of discuss it, Liz?" he said, gently.

"Oh, no need at all, dear," said Mum. "I've decided on her name."

"Well," began Dad, "I think there is."

"Me, too," I said. I had been left out of this for quite long enough.

"Really?" said Mum. "So far I've done ninety-nine percent of the work and I think I should be allowed to choose whatever name I want for *my* daughter."

"*Our* daughter," said Dad. "What then?"

"Josephine Munro Kenny," said Mum. "OK with you all?"

"Wow!" said Dad. "WOW!!"

"Whew!" I said. "WHEW!!"

"Josephine I like. Why on earth Munro?" asked Grandma. "Munro? Quite nice, I suppose, but strange."

"Oh," said Mum, waving her hands. "It's an old family name on her father's side."

"Funny," said Grandma. "First I ever heard of it. I know most of his family."

"Josephine Munro Kenny," said Mum, again. "OK Chas?"

"Cool as," I said. Boy, did I feel good.

At which point Josephine Munro Kenny woke up for another feed, and Mr. Magoo Two let us know it was time to get out of his cupboard.

About the Author

William Taylor lives in Raurimu, Mt. Ruapehu, New Zealand. His work is published worldwide, and Mr. Taylor's novel *Agnes the Sheep* won the prestigious Esther Glen Award in New Zealand for children's literature. His first book for Scholastic Hardcover was *Paradise Lane*. A former school-teacher, Mr. Taylor now writes full-time.